Becky + Frank's

Tigerbuttah

Deep inside the forest, amidst the tallest and oldest trees, stood a tiny cottage.

And inside that cottage lived a family of tigers.

The youngest tiger in this family was named Tigerbuttah!

Everyday he played
on a rope-swing with
his sister.

He pretended he
was a musketeer, swinging
from the mast of a great
pirate ship.

Today Tigerbuttah found it hard to imagine and even harder to pretend.

The ropes didn't feel like they were tied to a ship, the sticks didn't feel like mighty swords and the leaves were simply no fun at all.

Tigerbuttah sat down on the rug and told his parents.
"You're having trouble pretending?" queried Fatherbuttah.
"Oh no! And imagining?" exclaimed Motherbuttah.

"I was afraid this day would come, that's why I saved this special balloon," explained Fatherbuttah. "If you imagine as hard as you can, it can take you on countless adventures to faraway lands."

Tigerbuttah was so excited he ran out of the cottage as fast as he could, holding his balloon ever so tightly.

Why? Because in his mind the balloon was already as
big as his whole house, perhaps even the entire forest!

As quick as a hiccup the balloon took off into the sky, gliding upon the wind as if it were a giant bird.

"Goodbye, mother! Goodbye, father!" he shouted.

To which they replied in unison, "Goodbye, son! Be home before supper!"

"Good day," said a white cat, matter of factly, "I am Toothbrush Toyger, famous race-car driver, and I welcome you to the city of Monte Carlo!"

The automobile weaved through the city streets.

"You'd best hang on tight, we're driving this car all the way to China!" squealed Toothbrush Toyger, "Best of all, I know the perfect tour guide for you!"

Tigerbuttah was so excited that he began to giggle.

Upon his arrival in China, Tigerbuttah was warmly greeted by a husky Red Panda.

"I'm your big cousin Chinabuttah!" said the Red Panda. "Since we're celebrating, you should definitely wear this traditional tiger hat!"

"This is so cute and so are you!" replied Tigerbuttah.

With a little help, Tigerbuttah learned how to do the dragon dance.

Cousin Chinabuttah was very proud.

"Maybe my friend Tiki Tabby could teach you some other fine skills! You'll have to take your balloon... to Hawaii!" said a cheerful Chinabuttah.

Tiki Tabby certainly did teach Tigerbuttah a thing or two!

"Maybe when you're old enough you can use a board instead of a turtle!" he said.

"No way," said Tigerbuttah, "this turtle is my friend!"

Tigerbuttah let out a huge yawn for such a small tiger. "Sorry, I'm just so tired from all this pretending and imagining," said Tigerbuttah.

"It must have been a long day for you. You should probably get home for supper," replied Tiki Tabby.

Tigerbuttah once again set off in his balloon, waving goodbye to his new friends, who waved back from all over the world.

"Goodbye, Toothbrush Toyger! Goodbye, Gondola Kitten! Goodbye, Chinabuttah! Goodbye, Tiki Tabby!" he shouted from his balloon.

"Goodbye, Tigerbuttah! Come back soon!" they shouted in reply.

With one last burst of energy, Tigerbuttah ran through the forest towards his little cottage home.

"I can't wait to tell everyone about my adventures!" he said to himself.

To his surprise, his whole family was waiting for him outside.

"Welcome home!" said Fatherbuttah.

"I hope you had a good adventure," said Motherbuttah.

"I had the best adventure," gasped the little tiger, "but I think I've imagined enough for one day!"